GODZILLA™

ATTACK OF THE
BABY GODZILLAS

Adapted by Gina Shaw
Based on the screenplay written
by Dean Devlin & Roland Emmerich

SCHOLASTIC INC.

New York   Toronto   London   Auckland   Sydney

GODZILLA™

TriStar Pictures Presents

A CENTROPOLIS ENTERTAINMENT Production a FRIED FILMS and INDEPENDENT PICTURES Production a film by ROLAND EMMERICH MATTHEW BRODERICK JEAN RENO "GODZILLA" MARIA PITILLO HANK AZARIA KEVIN DUNN MICHAEL LERNER HARRY SHEARER creature designed by PATRICK TATOPOULOS visual effects supervisor VOLKER ENGEL music by DAVID ARNOLD co-executive producers ROB FRIED and CARY WOODS executive producers ROLAND EMMERICH · UTE EMMERICH · WILLIAM FAY based on the character "GODZILLA" owned and created by TOHO CO., LTD.
www.godzilla.com written by DEAN DEVLIN & ROLAND EMMERICH produced by DEAN DEVLIN directed by ROLAND EMMERICH SOUNDTRACK ON EPIC CDs AND CASSETTES

ISBN 0-590-68112-5

12 11 10 9 8 7 6 5 4   8 9/9 0 1 2 3/0

Designed by Joan Ferrigno

Printed in the U.S.A.

First Scholastic printing, June 1998

All was quiet — or as quiet as it gets in the middle of New York City. Then, suddenly, the ground began to shake. The earth quaked. People scattered in panic. The gigantic creature's scaly, clawed foot came down hard against the pavement, smashing cars and vans under its weight. The huge lizard let out a screeching wail. Godzilla had arrived in New York City!

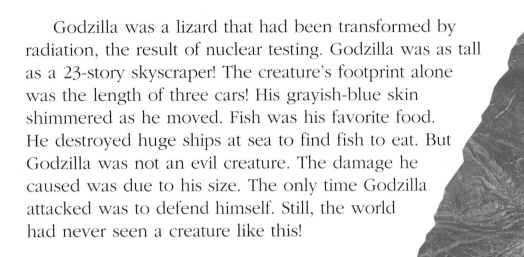

Godzilla was a lizard that had been transformed by radiation, the result of nuclear testing. Godzilla was as tall as a 23-story skyscraper! The creature's footprint alone was the length of three cars! His grayish-blue skin shimmered as he moved. Fish was his favorite food. He destroyed huge ships at sea to find fish to eat. But Godzilla was not an evil creature. The damage he caused was due to his size. The only time Godzilla attacked was to defend himself. Still, the world had never seen a creature like this!

Four people were hot on Godzilla's trail. Dr. Nick Tatopoulos was a scientific researcher. He studied animals that had been affected by radiation. Nick suspected that Godzilla was pregnant and might even have laid his eggs already! Some species, Nick knew, did not need a mate. They reproduced by themselves.

No one believed Nick's theory about the eggs — except Phillipe Roache. Phillipe and his team worked for the French Secret Service. They wanted to help destroy the titanic lizard. Their country's testing of nuclear bombs had created Godzilla and unleashed the reptile on the world. Nick teamed up with Phillipe and his crew to find Godzilla's eggs and destroy them all!

Audrey Timmonds and Victor "Animal" Palotti worked for a TV station in New York. Audrey was training to become a news reporter, and Animal was a cameraman. They both suspected that Nick and Phillipe knew something important about Godzilla. Audrey and Animal decided to follow them.

Nick and Phillipe's trail led to a huge arena in New York called Madison Square Garden. Godzilla had torn it to shreds! Dead fish were scattered everywhere — a sure sign that Godzilla had been there.

Cautiously, Nick, Phillipe, and Phillipe's men walked around inside the darkened building. They turned on their flashlights and jumped back at what they saw. Standing right in front of them were Godzilla's eggs. Each one was over nine feet tall! Long, mucuslike strands of brown liquid dripped from each of the shells.

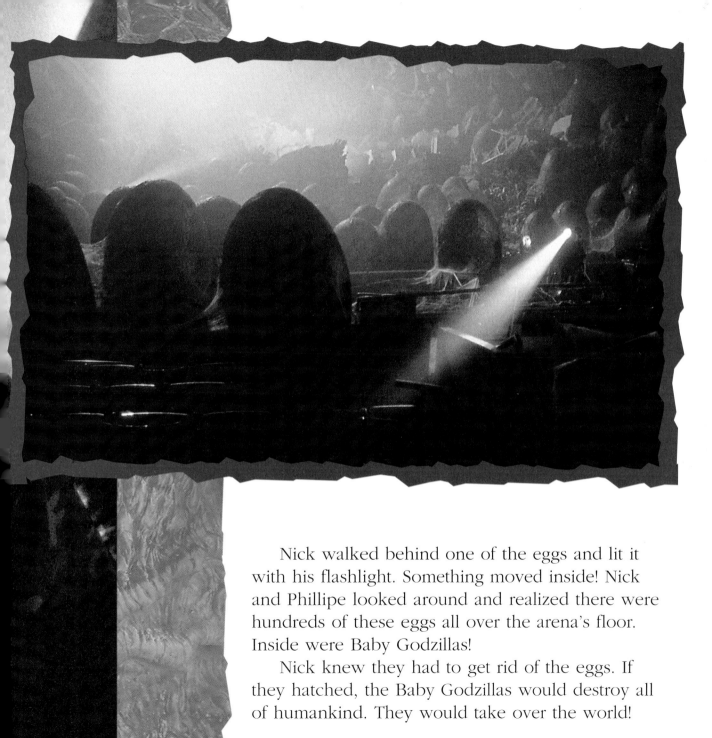

Nick walked behind one of the eggs and lit it with his flashlight. Something moved inside! Nick and Phillipe looked around and realized there were hundreds of these eggs all over the arena's floor. Inside were Baby Godzillas!

Nick knew they had to get rid of the eggs. If they hatched, the Baby Godzillas would destroy all of humankind. They would take over the world!

Together, Nick and Phillipe studied a group of eggs. Suddenly, Nick heard a loud crack! The shell ruptured and the egg rattled as the creature inside awakened. More cracking sounds filled the room as, one by one, eggs opened around the men!

Nick and Phillipe stared as the Baby Godzillas broke free of their shells. The brown, scaly beasts immediately gobbled up the dead fish that Godzilla had brought for them — just as Godzilla would have done. Nick and Phillipe turned pale. Slowly, they backed away from the hideous creatures. When they were far enough away, they *ran* for the exit!

At that moment, on a different level of the building, Animal and Audrey crawled out from a hole in the center of the floor. They were stunned to see hundreds of eggs, too! Animal picked up his camera and videotaped the hatching eggs. As Audrey nervously crept across the floor, an egg cracked. A scaly arm broke out through the shell and grabbed her leg. Audrey frantically kicked herself free and ran. Animal followed close behind.

Meanwhile, more and more Baby Godzillas frantically devoured the remaining fish. What would they eat when there were none left? Nick and Phillipe didn't want to find out. They raced through the hallways, stopping only to seal off doorways.

Phillipe turned to Nick and said, "Go and get help!"

Nick darted down the hallway, his heart pounding. Dozens of Baby Godzillas came around the corner, heading directly toward him. Nick knew he was trapped. Then, he spied an elevator. He ran to it, slamming his hand against the call button.

The Baby Godzillas sniffed the air and moved in toward Nick. They were coming at him from all sides. Panicked, Nick prayed the elevator would get there in time. At the last second, the elevator doors opened. Nick leaped inside.

He frantically pushed the "Close Door" button, but the doors reacted slowly. Was he a goner? As the doors finally began to close, a Baby Godzilla struck. Its head got caught in the closing doors. Petrified, Nick kicked the Baby Godzilla with all his might. It fell back and the doors closed. Nick breathed a deep sigh of relief! But he was still terrified. Would he ever be able to get away from these horrible beasts and get help?

On the next floor, the elevator doors opened again. Phillipe was standing guard. He swerved his gun around, ready to shoot. Frightened, Nick threw his hands up in the air. Then Phillipe recognized Nick.

"What happened?" Phillipe asked.

Nick answered, "They're all over the place. I couldn't get out."

Just then, the vent above them collapsed — and Audrey and Animal came tumbling down! Nick and Phillipe were shocked to see them. But there was no time to talk. Suddenly, all four heard a thumping sound growing louder and louder — the Baby Godzillas were coming closer!

Nick, Phillipe, Audrey, and Animal were trapped. They *had* to talk to the outside world.

"I know how you can get a message out of here," Audrey suddenly said.

If she could somehow get a live news report out, the whole world would know about the Baby Godzillas. She led the men into a broadcast booth. First they barricaded the door. Then Audrey turned on the computer and told everyone, "This is a direct line into our network's computer system." Audrey's TV station had covered sports events from this broadcast booth. They also monitored live news broadcasts from there.

At that moment, Animal turned on his video camera and pointed it at the Baby Godzillas clawing outside of the broadcast booth. Audrey began her report.

On TVs all over the city, she reported, "We're live from Madison Square Garden where Dr. Nick Tatopoulos has located Godzilla's nest. Doctor, tell us what is happening here."

Nick explained, "We've discovered over two hundred eggs, which began hatching only moments ago. If the military is listening, they *must immediately destroy this building* before the Baby Godzillas escape."

In no time, the computer beeped. Animal read the screen. "The good news is they got the message," he said. "The bad news is we've got five and a half minutes to get out of the building before it's bombed!"

Suddenly the room rocked as the Baby Godzillas began crashing against the blocked door. Phillipe jumped to his feet. He sprayed bullets into the front glass window, shattering it. Then he tossed a spool of cable out of the broken window. Animal slid down, followed by Phillipe, Nick, and Audrey. At that moment, the door gave out and the Baby Godzillas flooded into the room.

The team rushed out onto the escalators that led down to the main floor. They froze at the sight below. Hundreds of Baby Godzillas filled the lobby!

With only thirty seconds left, Phillipe spotted three large chandeliers hanging in a direct line between them and the front door. He fired at the first one. The chandelier dropped and shattered at the bottom of the escalator. The frightened Baby Godzillas scattered.

Phillipe led the way as they raced down the escalator. He made a path by shooting out the second, then the third chandelier. Each time, the Baby Godzillas backed away. Phillipe was the last one out. Audrey, Nick, and Animal were also safe. Sadly, however, no one from Phillipe's team survived.

The military's bomb hit its target and an enormous explosion erupted. It engulfed the entire building in a mountain of flames. Phillipe, Animal, Audrey, and Nick were thrown several yards forward, toppling onto the ground from the incredible impact. As the building crumbled in flames, many of the Baby Godzillas screamed. Soon they were silenced.

Slowly, Nick sat up and turned to Audrey. "Are you okay?" he asked. Audrey hugged Nick tightly.

Nick, Audrey, Animal, and Phillipe had survived. They were heroes for saving the world from the Baby Godzillas.

But Godzilla was still on the loose! And now that his babies had been destroyed, the huge lizard was filled with hatred and rage. Godzilla was out for revenge! Would anyone be able to stop him?